# The Sacrificial Code

How the Babylonian Bloodline Legion Influenced Fate

Disclaimer

The information and recipes contained in this book are based upon the research and the personal experiences of the author. It's for entertainment purposes only. It is not meant to replace any advice from a health care professional. This book is meant to compliment. The reader is encouraged to use good judgement when applying the information contained and to seek advice from a qualified professional if, and as needed. Professionals should be consulted as needed prior to undertaking any of the actions endorsed herein.

Every attempt has been made to provide accurate, up to date and reliable information. No warranties of any kind are expressed or implied. Readers acknowledge that the author is not engaging in the rendering of legal, financial, medical, or professional advice. By reading this, the reader agrees that under no circumstance the author is not responsible for any loss, direct or indirect, which is incurred by using this information contained within this book. Including but not limited to errors, omissions, or inaccuracies. This book is not intended as a replacement from what your health care provider has suggested. The author is not responsible for any adverse effects or consequences resulting from the use of any of the suggestions, preparations or procedures discussed in this book. All matters pertaining to your health should be supervised by a health care professional. I am not a doctor, or a medical professional nor do I play one on TV. This book is designed as an educational and entertainment tool only. Please always check with your health practitioner before taking any vitamins, supplements, diet change, or herbs, as they may have side-effects, especially when combined with medications, alcohol, or other vitamins or supplements.  All rights reserved. No part of this publication may be reproduced, distributed, or transmitted in any form or by any means, including photo copying, or recording, or other electronic, or mechanical methods, without the prior written permission of the author, except in the case of brief quotations, embodied in critical reviews, in certain other noncommercial uses permitted by copyright laws. Although every precaution has been taken by the author to verify the accuracy of the information contained herein, the author assumes no responsibility for any errors, or omissions. No liability is assumed for damages that may result from the information that is obtained within. The author declares that the research was conducted in the absence of any commercial or financial relationships that could be construed as a potential conflict of interest. This declaration is deemed fair and valid by both the American Bar association and the committee of publishers' association and is legally binding throughout the world.

By purchasing this book, you are consenting to its contents. It is important to note that the author of this book is not an expert on the topics discussed within, and any recommendations or suggestions made are for entertainment purposes only. It is recommended that professionals be consulted before taking any actions discussed in this book. This declaration has been deemed fair and valid by the American Bar Association and the Committee of Publishers' Association and is legally binding worldwide. The information contained in this book is considered truthful and accurate, and any use or misuse of the information is solely at the reader's discretion. The author cannot be held liable for any hardship or damages that may result from the reader's actions after reading this book.

A.L. Childers

Copyrighted Material

Copyright 2023 Audrey Childers.

This book, or parts thereof, may not be reproduced in any form without the written permission from the Author. All rights reserved. This book is copyright protected. You cannot sell, distribute, use, quote or paraphrase any part or the content within this book without the author. Legal action will be pursued if breached.

All rights reserved. In accordance with the U.S. write copyright act of 1976, the scanning, the uploading, and electronic scanning of any part of this book. Without permission of the publisher or author constitutes unlawful piracy and theft of the author's intellectual property. If you would like to use material from this book. (Other than for review purposes), prior written permission must be obtained by contacting the author @ permissions @ audreychilders@hotmail.com. Thank you for your support of the author's rights.   All the data, research and references are sited in the back of the book, and it does back up all claims that have been discussed by the author.

All the data, research, footnotes, and references are cited in the back of the book, and it does back up all claims that have been discussed by the author. The internet is a valuable source of information, but unlike printed works, it cannot be relied upon for long-term reference. News articles may be removed from their websites, and data that you have cited may be erased, or the websites may have been terminated. This represents a challenge to authors who want to document the origin of their information.

Dear readers, it is important to take all necessary precautions before undertaking any DIY project. Always follow the instructions and be extra careful when creating your own homemade products. It is never a good idea to stretch yourself too thin. Remember that every fabric or material may react differently to suggested use. While this is a non-toxic and natural way to clean your home, it is always recommended to wear protective gloves and eyewear. Please note that although every effort has been made to provide you with the best possible information, neither the publisher nor the author is responsible for any accidents, injuries, or damage incurred because of tasks performed by readers. The author will not assume any responsibility for personal or property damage resulting from the formulas found in this book. It is important to keep in mind that this book is separate from professional services.

Authors note:

Please note that any reference or resemblance to any person or organization in this book, whether living or dead, existing, or defunct, is purely coincidental. I want to remind all readers that all rights are reserved and no part of this book or any associated ancillary materials may be reproduced or transmitted in any form by any means, electronic or mechanical, including photocopying, recording, duplicating, or by any informational storage or retrieval system, without express written permission from the author. It is important to respect the author's intellectual property and adhere to copyright laws.

A note of caution:

Prioritizing your own health and well-being is essential for a fulfilling life. I firmly believe that self-care and personal health empowerment are powerful tools, and that everyone should take the initiative to improve their own understanding. The more knowledge you have, the more control you have over your own health. However, it's important to remember that consulting with a trained medical professional is always necessary in cases of long-standing and undiagnosed symptoms. This book is not intended to replace professional medical judgment but can certainly serve as a valuable supplement to it. Stay informed and vigilant, but always remember to seek professional advice when needed. Please note that the information provided in this book is for educational and entertainment purposes only, and no warranty is given concerning the accuracy of this information. Be smart, be sensible, and prioritize your health by utilizing good common sense. Above all else, be kind and compassionate towards yourself, your body, and your mind.

An entity is different and specific to each individual or item to which it has attached itself. As to alternative forms of medicine or healing, the author of this book has yet to offer any promised outcomes. Some human issues are more profound than cleansing a new home or spiritual entity possession and removal. Therefore, you must understand that this isn't a quick fix for issues that may have gone on in your or someone else's life. Cleansing a new home or spiritual entity possession and removal is not designed as a replacement for traditional psychological and medical treatment or advice, and it is not intended to treat, diagnose, cure, or prevent any disease. There is a difference between entity removal, energy healing, deep-rooted physiological issues, and demonic possession. If you or someone you know seems to have signs of demonic activity, you should contact a priest for counsel and prayer. In addition, with the corporation and aid of a medical professional, they can help you discern if the symptoms have a more natural cause, physiological or physical. A priest can perform exorcisms if no such reasons can be clearly identified or if they seem to be occupied by a spirit. We don't need special authorization to perform deliverance prayers on a person, place, or object, but if it is an exorcism, you must have someone skilled and trained to perform it correctly.

All in all, a spiritual entity possession and entity attachment removal is not something you merely play around with. A demon will eat your lunch and pop that bag right before you.

As befitted in nature and a world that cannot be seen with human eyes, the author is protected by a binding spell of any malicious intent. Any dark or evil force may return to its source, shield my home, health, heart, and mind, as this includes all family, friends, objects, and animals of mine, as we remain free, always safe, and well indeed. You are bound to return to your source with flight; I banish thee with this holy light.

Dear Creator, please grant me your protection from those who attempt to justify evil actions as good and twist truth into lies to achieve their malicious intentions. I ask that you guard me and my loved ones against any forms of deceit and schemes against righteousness. May we be surrounded by the purest vibrations and a sphere of White Light that encompasses every corner, crack, and shelter of our dwellings. Please keep this sphere of White Light free from any negative or harmful energies, especially those of demonic origin. I also request that this sphere of White Light be expanded to cover the space that we always inhabit, ensuring our safety and well-being. Thank you for your guidance and protection.

# Introduction:

In this journey through the pages of "The Sacrificial Code: How the Babylonian Bloodline Legion Influenced Fate," we will look deep into the ancient secrets and machinations of the enigmatic Bloodline Legion. We will explore how this secretive group has influenced the course of history, determining who among us is destined for sacrifice. But fear not, for this is not a tale of despair, but rather a call to action, a guide to liberating humanity from the chains of this bloodline tyranny.

Throughout history, the Bloodline Legion has exercised its power over our lives, deciding who will thrive and who will perish. Their influence has been pervasive, shaping the destinies of nations, families, and individuals. However, armed with the knowledge we have gained, we can now begin to dismantle this oppressive system and take control of our own fate.

First and foremost, it is essential to understand the mechanisms by which the Bloodline Legion operates. By studying their rituals, symbols, and hidden codes, we can decipher their strategies and identify their members. Knowledge is power, and in this case, it is the key to our liberation.

We must unite as a collective force against this bloodline tyranny. Humanity, in all its diversity, must stand together, breaking free from the divisions created by the Bloodline Legion. Only through solidarity can we hope to challenge their dominance and pave the way for a future where all individuals are valued and recognized for their unique contributions.

The Bloodline Legion has woven a web of control over humanity, but it is a story that can be rewritten. By reclaiming our individual and collective power, we can forge a new path, one that is free from the shackles of bloodline determinism.

"The Sacrificial Code" serves as a wake-up call, urging humanity to rise up and liberate itself from the chains of the Bloodline Legion. It is a call to action, a roadmap for reclaiming our destinies and shaping a future where every individual has the opportunity to thrive. Together, let us break free from the influence of the ancient Babylonian legion of bloodlines and create a world where our fate is truly in our own hands.

# Chapter 1: The Ancient Babylonian Bloodline Legion Revealed

## The Origins of the Babylonian Bloodline Legion

Throughout history, countless mysterious organizations have existed, shaping the course of humanity behind closed doors. One such enigmatic group is the Babylonian Bloodline Legion. This subchapter delves into the origins of this secretive legion and its profound influence on the fate of humanity.

The Babylonian Bloodline Legion traces its roots back to the ancient civilizations of Mesopotamia. In the heart of the legendary city of Babylon, a group of influential families formed a clandestine alliance, bound by bloodlines that were believed to possess extraordinary powers. These families, known as the "Babylonian Bloodlines," held a deep-seated belief that they were direct descendants of gods, chosen to guide and control the destiny of humanity.

Within the Babylonian Bloodline Legion, a complex system was established to determine who would be sacrificed to appease the gods and maintain the balance of power. Through meticulous rituals and ceremonies, the legion analyzed the lives of individuals, seeking signs and omens that would reveal their suitability for sacrifice. This process involved scrutinizing various factors, including lineage, social status, and even astrological alignments.

Over the centuries, the Babylonian Bloodline Legion evolved, adapting to the changing times while preserving its core beliefs. As empires rose and fell, the legion's influence expanded beyond the borders of Babylon, infiltrating other civilizations and power structures. Their knowledge and practices were passed down through generations, ensuring the continuity of their legacy.

It is important to note that the Babylonian Bloodline Legion's power doesn't solely lie in their ability to decide who is to be sacrificed. Their influence extends far beyond, affecting the rise and fall of nations, economic systems, and even individual destinies. The legion has been said to manipulate events, pulling the strings from the shadows, all to fulfill their own agenda and maintain their grip on power.

Today, the Babylonian Bloodline Legion remains shrouded in secrecy, hidden in plain sight. While their methods may have adapted to the modern world, their ultimate goal remains the same – to influence the course of human fate, ensuring their continued dominance.

The Babylonian Bloodline Legion's origins can be traced back to the ancient city of Babylon. This secretive organization has exerted its influence over humanity for centuries, using intricate rituals and ceremonies to determine who is to be sacrificed. However, their power extends far beyond this, impacting the rise and fall of nations and shaping the destiny of individuals. The legacy of the Babylonian Bloodline Legion persists, as they continue to manipulate events from the shadows, preserving their hold on power and shaping the course of humanity's fate.

## The Hidden Influence of the Bloodlines throughout History

In the annals of human history, there exists a pervasive but often overlooked force that has shaped the course of civilizations: the ancient Babylonian bloodline legion. These enigmatic bloodlines have played a significant role in determining who is to be sacrificed, directly influencing the fate of humanity itself. In this subchapter, we will delve into the depths of this hidden influence, exploring the ways in which these bloodlines have shaped our world and continue to do so today.

## Unveiling the Veiled Machinations:

Throughout the ages, the Babylonian bloodline legion has exerted their influence by meticulously orchestrating the rituals of sacrifice. These rituals, shrouded in secrecy, have been used to consolidate power, maintain control over nations, and manipulate the destinies of individuals. By exploring the ancient art of sacrifice, we can begin to comprehend the hidden motives and agendas behind these bloodlines.

## The Historical Echoes:

From ancient Mesopotamia to the present day, the echoes of this bloodline influence can be observed in the rise and fall of empires, the manipulation of political landscapes, and the control of economic systems. By tracing the lineage of these bloodlines, we can uncover the intricate web of connections that stretches across time and space, transcending borders and cultures.

## Unmasking the Power Players:

Within the ranks of the Babylonian bloodline legion, certain individuals have risen to prominence as power players, wielding their influence over the masses. From monarchs and religious leaders to influential figures in finance and media, these bloodlines have carefully selected those who will perpetuate their legacy and ensure their continued control. By understanding who these power players are, we can gain insight into the mechanisms of influence that shape our world.

**The Modern-Day Impact:**

Though ancient in origin, the influence of the Babylonian bloodline legion remains palpable in the present day. By examining the subtle but pervasive ways in which these bloodlines continue to shape our societies, we can become more aware of the forces at play in our lives. From the decisions made by world leaders to the direction of global events, the hidden hand of these bloodlines can be discerned if one knows where to look.

We have dug into the enigmatic world of the Babylonian bloodline legion, uncovering their hidden influence throughout history. By understanding the power dynamics and mechanisms employed by these bloodlines, we can begin to grasp the profound impact they have had on shaping the fate of humanity. As we continue to explore their machinations, we must question who truly holds the reins of power and strive to reclaim our own destinies from the clutches of these ancient bloodlines.

## Unraveling the Secrets of the Bloodline Legion

In the vast annals of human history, there exists a hidden truth that has shaped the destiny of nations and individuals alike. This truth, concealed within the depths of time, is the enigmatic Bloodline Legion of ancient Babylon. For centuries, this secretive group has held the power to determine who shall be sacrificed, influencing the course of human fate in ways unimaginable to the common eye.

"The Sacrificial Code: How the Babylonian Bloodline Legion Influenced Fate" explores the mysteries surrounding this clandestine organization, shedding light on their origins, methods, and the profound impact they have had on the grand tapestry of human existence.

"Unraveling the Secrets of the Bloodline Legion," really got into the heart of their operations, revealing the hidden mechanisms through which they decide who is to be sacrificed. The bloodlines, tracing their ancestry back to the ancient Babylonian empire, possess an unparalleled understanding of the intricacies of power and control. Through generations of careful observation, manipulation, and influence, they have honed their craft, becoming masters of destiny.

The chapter explores the archaic rituals, esoteric knowledge, and intricate web of connections that allow the Bloodline Legion to select their sacrificial victims. Their decisions are not arbitrary; rather, they are based on a complex system of factors, including lineage, societal influence, and hidden allegiances. Unveiling this process sheds light on the inner workings of this shadowy organization and unravels the mysteries that have perplexed humanity for millennia.

However, "Unraveling the Secrets of the Bloodline Legion" does not merely expose the truth; it also aims to empower humanity. By understanding the forces that have shaped our lives, we can better navigate the invisible currents of power that flow beneath the surface. This knowledge allows us to question the systems that govern our societies and seek a more equitable and just world.

"The Sacrificial Code: How the Babylonian Bloodline Legion Influenced Fate" offers a rare glimpse into the hidden world of the Bloodline Legion. Through its subchapter, "Unraveling the Secrets of the Bloodline Legion," readers are invited to delve into the mysterious mechanisms through which the ancient Babylonian legion of bloodlines decides who is to be sacrificed. This knowledge empowers humanity to challenge the status quo and strive for a future free from the invisible chains that have bound us for far too long.

# Chapter 2: The Sacrificial Code Unveiled

## Understanding the Concept of Sacrifice in Babylonian Culture

The ancient Babylonian civilization holds a captivating allure for historians, archaeologists, and enthusiasts of ancient cultures. Among the many intriguing aspects of this civilization, the concept of sacrifice stands out as a fascinating and enigmatic practice. In this subchapter, we will dig into the depths of Babylonian culture to explore the profound meaning and significance of sacrifice in their society.

Sacrifice, in the Babylonian context, was a ritualistic act that held immense importance in their religious and social fabric. It was believed that by offering sacrifices, individuals could forge a connection with the divine and appease the gods. These rituals were seen as a way to maintain harmony and order within the cosmos, ensuring the continued prosperity of their civilization.

The Babylonian bloodline legion played a crucial role in determining who would be sacrificed and when. This select group, comprising the highest-ranking members of society, possessed a deep understanding of the cosmic forces and their influence on human fate. By studying celestial events, divination, and interpreting signs, they were able to discern the will of the gods and determine the sacrificial recipients.

It is important to note that sacrifice in Babylonian culture was not limited to humans alone. Animals, such as sheep, goats, and cattle, were also offered to the gods. This practice symbolized the transfer of impurities or sins from the human realm to the divine realm. By sacrificing these animals, individuals sought purification and atonement for their transgressions.

The Babylonians firmly believed that sacrifice was a reciprocal act between humans and the gods. It was believed that by giving up something of value, humans could expect blessings, protection, and divine intervention in return. Sacrifice was seen as a means of establishing a symbiotic relationship with the gods, ensuring their favor and benevolence.

Understanding the concept of sacrifice in Babylonian culture allows us to gain a deeper insight into the religious and societal dynamics of this ancient civilization. It highlights the significance they placed on maintaining cosmic harmony and the lengths to which they would go to appease the gods. By comprehending their beliefs and practices, we can better appreciate the complexities of Babylonian culture and its enduring influence on human history.

This subchapter aims to shed light on the intricate workings of the Babylonian bloodline legion and their role in determining sacrificial recipients. By exploring their methods of divination and interpreting celestial events, we can begin to unravel the mysteries surrounding this ancient practice. So, join us on this captivating journey into the heart of Babylonian sacrifice and discover how it influenced the fate of individuals and the destiny of their civilization.

## The Rituals and Ceremonies of the Bloodline Legion

In the dark corners of history, an ancient Babylonian legion known as the Bloodline Legion has wielded an immense influence over the fate of humanity. This secretive group, shrouded in mystery and steeped in ancient rituals and ceremonies, holds the power to determine who is to be sacrificed, altering the course of destiny itself. In this subchapter, we delve deep into the enigmatic practices of the Bloodline Legion, shedding light on their arcane rituals and unveiling the truth behind their decision-making process.

Central to the Bloodline Legion's power is their mastery of rituals that have been passed down through generations. These rituals, conducted in hidden chambers and sacred spaces, are believed to channel the ancient Babylonian spirits that guide their choices. From the moment of initiation, new members of the Legion participate in these ceremonies, binding themselves to an ancient pact that compels them to carry out the will of their bloodline ancestors.

One such ritual is the "Rite of the Ancestors," where members commune with the spirits of their forefathers. Through intricate incantations and offerings, they seek guidance and receive visions that reveal the identities of those who are destined to be sacrificed. This ritual serves as a pivotal moment for Legion members, as it strengthens their connection to their bloodline heritage and solidifies their commitment to their sacred duty.

Another essential ceremony is the "Scrying of the Bloodlines," a divination practice that enables the Legion to discern the hidden patterns and connections between individuals. By studying the intricate web of bloodlines, the Legion identifies those who possess the necessary traits and qualities for sacrifice. This meticulous process involves ancient texts, astrological charts, and the deciphering of cryptic symbols, all of which combine to reveal the chosen ones.

The decision-making process of the Bloodline Legion goes beyond mere rituals and ceremonies. It is rooted in a complex system of lineage, genetics, and prophecy. Through careful examination of

## The Rituals and Ceremonies of the Bloodline Legion

In the dark corners of history, an ancient Babylonian legion known as the Bloodline Legion has wielded an immense influence over the fate of humanity. This secretive group, shrouded in mystery and steeped in ancient rituals and ceremonies, holds the power to determine who is to be sacrificed, altering the course of destiny itself. In this subchapter, we delve deep into the enigmatic practices of the Bloodline Legion, shedding light on their arcane rituals and unveiling the truth behind their decision-making process.

Central to the Bloodline Legion's power is their mastery of rituals that have been passed down through generations. These rituals, conducted in hidden chambers and sacred spaces, are believed to channel the ancient Babylonian spirits that guide their choices. From the moment of initiation, new members of the Legion participate in these ceremonies, binding themselves to an ancient pact that compels them to carry out the will of their bloodline ancestors.

One such ritual is the "Rite of the Ancestors," where members commune with the spirits of their forefathers. Through intricate incantations and offerings, they seek guidance and receive visions that reveal the identities of those who are destined to be sacrificed. This ritual serves as a pivotal moment for Legion members, as it strengthens their connection to their bloodline heritage and solidifies their commitment to their sacred duty.

Another essential ceremony is the "Scrying of the Bloodlines," a divination practice that enables the Legion to discern the hidden patterns and connections between individuals. By studying the intricate web of bloodlines, the Legion identifies those who possess the necessary traits and qualities for sacrifice. This meticulous process involves ancient texts, astrological charts, and the deciphering of cryptic symbols, all of which combine to reveal the chosen ones.

The decision-making process of the Bloodline Legion goes beyond mere rituals and ceremonies. It is rooted in a complex system of lineage, genetics, and prophecy. Through careful examination of bloodlines, the Legion seeks to identify those who possess the potential to influence the course of history. They believe that sacrifice is necessary to maintain the delicate balance between fate and free will, ensuring that humanity's destiny unfolds according to their ancient design.

The rituals and ceremonies of the Bloodline Legion are deeply ingrained in the fabric of their existence. Through their enigmatic practices, they claim the power to determine who will be sacrificed, ultimately shaping the course of human history. The mysteries surrounding their decision-making process are finally unveiled, shedding light on the ancient Babylonian influence that continues to resonate in our world today.

## Deciphering the Symbols and Codes of Sacrificial Selection

In our quest to understand the ancient Babylonian bloodline legion and their influence on fate, it is crucial to delve into the intricate world of symbols and codes that governed their sacrificial selection process. This subchapter aims to shed light on this mysterious realm, providing insights into how the ancient Babylonians determined who would be offered as a sacrifice.

Symbols played a paramount role in the sacrificial selection process. The Babylonians believed that certain symbols held immense power and could reveal the destinies of individuals. These symbols, often engraved on stone tablets or woven into intricate tapestries, were carefully studied and interpreted by the priesthood. Through a complex system of symbolism, they sought to unravel the divine messages embedded within these mystical signs.

Decoding these symbols required a deep understanding of the cosmic forces at play. The Babylonian bloodline legion believed that the positioning of celestial bodies and the alignment of stars held the key to unlocking the secrets of sacrifice. Astrological charts were meticulously analyzed to determine the auspicious moments for conducting sacrifices and identifying suitable candidates.

Codes, on the other hand, were used to veil the true intentions of the Babylonian bloodline legion. These codes acted as a form of protection, ensuring that their rituals remained concealed from those outside their inner circle. The priesthood developed a sophisticated language of codes, only known to the initiated, that allowed them to communicate their intentions covertly. This secrecy ensured that the sacrificial selection process remained hidden from prying eyes, safeguarding the power of the bloodline legion.

Understanding the symbols and codes of sacrificial selection is essential in comprehending the immense influence the ancient Babylonian bloodline legion wielded over fate. By deciphering these intricate messages, we gain a glimpse into the inner workings of their rituals and the criteria upon which sacrifices were chosen.

As we search deeper into this book, we will explore the symbolic language used by the Babylonians, examining the significance of celestial alignments and the hidden meanings behind their coded messages. By unraveling the secrets of the symbols and codes of sacrificial selection, we hope to shed light on the enigmatic practices of the Babylonian bloodline legion and their lasting impact on the course of human history.

Join us on this journey of exploration as we strive to unlock the mysteries of the ancient Babylonian bloodline legion and their profound influence on the destiny of humanity.

# Chapter 3: The Role of Bloodlines in Determining Sacrificial Candidates

## The Criteria for Sacrificial Selection by the Bloodline Legion

In the enigmatic world of ancient Babylon, a secretive and powerful group known as the Bloodline Legion held sway over the destiny of humanity. Their influence was far-reaching, shaping the course of events through a practice that sent shivers down the spine of every citizen - sacrificial selection. In this subchapter, we delve deep into the hidden criteria used by the Babylonian Bloodline Legion to determine who would become a sacrificial offering, shedding light on a dark chapter of human history.

To the average person, the concept of being chosen for sacrifice was a terrifying prospect. The knowledge that the Bloodline Legion had the power to decide who would be offered up to the gods created an atmosphere of fear and trepidation. But what factors guided their selection process? How did they choose who would be sacrificed?

First and foremost, the Bloodline Legion prioritized bloodline purity. Ancient Babylonians believed that the gods favored those with untainted lineage, tracing back generations. As such, individuals from prestigious families were more likely to be selected for sacrifice. The notion of divine favor bestowed upon those with noble ancestry played a significant role in determining who would be offered up to the gods.

Additionally, physical attributes and health conditions were crucial in the selection process. The Babylonians believed that their gods demanded perfection, and thus, only those who possessed flawless physical traits were considered worthy of sacrifice. Individuals with physical deformities or illnesses were deemed unfit to serve as offerings and were spared from the dark fate that awaited others.

Furthermore, the Bloodline Legion evaluated the individual's character and behavior. Only those who displayed unwavering loyalty to the Babylonian empire and adhered strictly to societal norms were deemed suitable for sacrifice. Disloyalty, rebellion, or any indication of deviant behavior would disqualify an individual from consideration.

While these criteria provided a general framework, the selection process was not entirely rigid. The Bloodline Legion possessed a certain degree of discretion and could make exceptions or prioritize certain individuals based on their personal judgment. Factors such as political alliances, strategic considerations, or even bribery could sway their decisions, revealing the complex and intricate web of power that governed sacrificial selection.

In conclusion, the Babylonian Bloodline Legion's criteria for sacrificial selection were rooted in bloodline purity, physical perfection, and unwavering loyalty. These factors, intertwined with personal judgment and strategic considerations, played a profound role in determining who would be offered up to the gods. As we unravel the mysteries surrounding the ancient Babylonian empire, we come to understand the mechanisms that shaped the destinies of countless individuals and influenced the course of human history.

The Manipulation of Fate through Bloodline Influence

In the annals of history, the ancient Babylonian civilization stands as a testament to the depths of human ingenuity and ambition. But behind the glittering façade of this mighty empire lies a dark secret, one that has remained hidden for centuries: the manipulation of fate through bloodline influence. In our book, "The Sacrificial Code: How the Babylonian Bloodline Legion Influenced Fate," we delve deep into the inner workings of this enigmatic legion and expose their intricate methods of deciding who is to be sacrificed.

To understand the true significance of bloodline influence, one must first comprehend the Babylonian belief in the interconnectedness of blood and destiny. According to their ancient texts, certain bloodlines were deemed more sacred than others, possessing a direct line to the gods themselves. These chosen few held immense power and authority, capable of shaping the course of history through their influence over fate.

Our book reveals the meticulous rituals and practices employed by the Babylonian bloodline legion to decipher the will of the gods. Through intricate divination techniques, they would study the lineage of individuals, tracing their bloodline back generations, and determining their suitability for sacrifice. This macabre selection process was not arbitrary but based on a complex system of signs and symbols, meticulously recorded over centuries.

But what motivated this powerful legion to manipulate fate through bloodline influence? Our research suggests that it was an insatiable hunger for power and control. By determining who would be sacrificed, they could ensure their own prosperity and longevity. The ancient Babylonian empire thrived on the belief that their actions were sanctioned by the gods, legitimizing their rule and suppressing dissent.

However, it is not enough to simply expose this hidden history. We must also examine how the manipulation of fate through bloodline influence continues to impact humanity today. The remnants of this ancient practice can be seen in the world's power structures, where certain bloodlines still hold disproportionate influence and control. By understanding the origins of this manipulation, we can begin to challenge and dismantle these unjust systems.

"The Sacrificial Code" is not just a historical account but a call to action for humanity. It is a reminder that we have the power to shape our own destinies, free from the constraints of bloodline influence. By exposing the secrets of the Babylonian bloodline legion, we hope to empower individuals to question and challenge the forces that seek to control their fate.

In conclusion, the manipulation of fate through bloodline influence is a dark chapter in history, one that continues to impact humanity today. Through our book, "The Sacrificial Code," we invite you to embark on a journey of discovery, to unveil the secrets of the ancient Babylonian bloodline legion, and to reclaim your own agency in shaping your destiny. It is time to break free from the chains of the past and forge a future where each individual's worth is not determined by their bloodline, but by their actions and character.

## Examining the Psychological Impact on Sacrificial Candidates

In the enigmatic realm of ancient Babylon, the bloodline legion held an unprecedented influence over the fate of humanity. Delving into the depths of this intriguing subject, we inevitably encounter the psychological impact on those chosen as sacrificial candidates. This subchapter aims to shed light on the profound effects experienced by these individuals as they grappled with their impending sacrifice.

The ancient Babylonian legion of bloodlines possessed an intricate system for determining who would be offered as a sacrifice. This mystifying process, guided by divination and elaborate rituals, often left the chosen candidates filled with a spectrum of emotions. Fear, anxiety, and despair were prevalent amongst them, as they were faced with the inevitability of their own demise.

The psychological impact on sacrificial candidates can be viewed through the lens of existential dread. Confronted with the grim reality of their impending sacrifice, they were forced to confront their mortality in the most profound way imaginable. This existential crisis often led to a deep introspection regarding the purpose and meaning of their lives, as they grappled with the notion of being mere pawns in the cosmic chessboard of destiny.

Furthermore, sacrificial candidates also experienced a sense of isolation and abandonment. The knowledge that they were chosen to appease the bloodline legion created a mental and emotional chasm between them and their fellow humans. They became outcasts, shunned by society, and burdened with the weight of their impending sacrifice. This isolation intensified their psychological trauma, leading to a sense of despair and hopelessness.

However, amidst the darkness, some sacrificial candidates also experienced a profound transformation. The impending sacrifice forced them to confront their deepest fears and embrace their mortality. In this crucible of existential crisis, a select few found a renewed sense of purpose and spiritual enlightenment. They transcended their mortal constraints and accepted their fate, becoming beacons of courage and wisdom for the wider human community.

In conclusion, the psychological impact on sacrificial candidates chosen by the ancient Babylonian bloodline legion was a multi-faceted phenomenon. It encompassed existential dread, isolation, and introspection, but also offered the potential for spiritual growth. As we examine this aspect of the sacrificial code, we gain a greater understanding of the complex interplay between fate, human psychology, and the enigmatic forces that shaped ancient Babylonian civilization.

# Chapter 4: The Modern-Day Influence of the Babylonian Bloodline Legion

## Tracing the Bloodlines in Contemporary Society

Throughout history, bloodlines have played a significant role in shaping the destiny of individuals and societies. In this subchapter, "Tracing the Bloodlines in Contemporary Society," we examine the intriguing world of the ancient Babylonian bloodline legion and its influence on fate. Addressed to humanity, particularly those fascinated by the enigmatic workings of ancient civilizations and the secrets behind the selection of sacrificial victims, this chapter aims to shed light on a hidden aspect of our collective history.

The Babylonian bloodline legion, an elite group of individuals with a lineage tracing back to the ancient Mesopotamian empire, holds a power that extends far beyond what meets the eye. As we explore their influence in contemporary society, we begin to unravel the intricate web they have woven, spanning generations and continents. This subchapter seeks to unveil their methods and the criteria they employ to determine who is to be sacrificed.

Examining the labyrinthine connections that these bloodlines have established, we discover that their influence extends into the realms of politics, finance, and culture. From the corridors of power to the boardrooms of multinational corporations, their presence is subtle but unmistakable. By tracing the genealogical lines, we can uncover the hidden mechanisms that facilitate their control over society.

Yet our exploration does not stop at mere observation. We dig deeper into the motives and rituals that drive these bloodlines' sacrificial practices. By understanding their ancient beliefs and the significance they attach to these acts, we gain insight into their worldview and the reasons behind their continued influence. It becomes clear that these rituals are not arbitrary but rather deeply rooted in the Babylonian tradition, perpetuating the cycle of power and control.

As we navigate this intriguing terrain, it is crucial to approach the subject with an open mind. The aim is not to promote conspiracy theories or endorse any particular agenda but rather to provide a comprehensive examination of an often-overlooked aspect of our past. By doing so, we empower ourselves with knowledge and understanding, enabling us to make informed choices about the future.

"Tracing the Bloodlines in Contemporary Society" invites humanity to explore the hidden forces that shape our lives and destinies. By unraveling the intricate connections of the Babylonian bloodline legion, we gain a deeper understanding of the world we inhabit. It is through this understanding that we can begin to question, challenge, and ultimately reshape the systems that govern us.

### The Subtle Manipulation of Power and Control

In the depths of history, an ancient Babylonian bloodline legion emerged, weaving a web of power and control that continues to permeate our world today. This subchapter delves into the intricacies of their methods and sheds light on how they decide who is to be sacrificed, ultimately influencing the very fabric of our fates.

Throughout the ages, power has been sought after, coveted, and clung to by those who desire control over others. The ancient Babylonian bloodline legion understood this all too well. They harnessed their knowledge of human psychology, exploiting the human need for security, belonging, and purpose. Through subtle manipulation, they have ensured their continued dominance over humanity.

This legion of bloodlines possesses an intricate network of influence, spanning across various sectors and institutions. They carefully select key individuals to be groomed for positions of power, shaping the course of nations and societies. Their selection process is a combination of bloodline heritage, loyalty, and the willingness to carry out their hidden agenda.

To maintain their control, this ancient legion employs a range of tactics, operating beneath the surface of our collective awareness. They utilize the media, shaping public opinion through carefully crafted narratives and controlling the information flow. By controlling the narrative, they manipulate the masses, ensuring conformity and obedience.

Furthermore, the Babylonian bloodline legion understands the power of fear. They manufacture crises, instilling a sense of urgency and chaos, which allows them to exert control over the populace. By carefully orchestrating events, they guide humanity towards their desired outcomes, all while remaining hidden in the shadows.

Their influence extends beyond the political realm, infiltrating religious institutions, financial systems, and even the entertainment industry. By controlling these pillars of society, they shape the thoughts, beliefs, and behaviors of the masses. Their ultimate goal is to maintain a system of control that ensures their continued dominance over humanity.

It is crucial for us, as humanity, to awaken to these subtle manipulations and break free from their grasp. By recognizing the hidden hands that shape our world, we can begin to reclaim our individual and collective power. Through knowledge and awareness, we can expose their schemes, dismantling their control and creating a future based on freedom, equality, and justice.

The time has come for humanity to rise above the influence of the ancient Babylonian bloodline legion. We must unite, empower one another, and work towards a world where power is no longer concentrated in the hands of the few. By doing so, we can rewrite the narrative of our fate, forging a path towards a brighter and more equitable future.

**Uncovering the Connections between Sacrifices and Global Events**

Throughout history, there have been countless reports and legends surrounding the mysterious connection between sacrifices and global events. From ancient civilizations to modern times, the practice of sacrificing individuals to appease the gods or alter the course of fate has been prevalent in various forms. In this subchapter, we delve deep into the intriguing world of sacrifice and its undeniable influence on global events, drawing particular attention to the ancient

Babylonian bloodline legion that has played a significant role in determining who is to be sacrificed.

The Babylonian Bloodline Legion, an enigmatic group believed to have originated in ancient Mesopotamia, has long been associated with the intricate workings of fate. This secretive legion is said to possess the knowledge and power to discern which individuals must be sacrificed to maintain balance and influence the unfolding of events on a global scale. Delving into their ancient texts and rituals, we begin to unravel the intricate web they weave to shape the course of human destiny.

One cannot deny the correlation between sacrifices and significant global events throughout history. From the rise and fall of empires to natural disasters and even political regimes, sacrifices have often been used as a means to affect change and manipulate the outcome of these events. By exploring case studies from various cultures and time periods, we can begin to see the patterns and connections that exist between sacrifices and the resulting global repercussions.

It is essential to approach this topic with a critical mind, questioning the legitimacy and ethics of such practices. Are sacrifices truly necessary, or do they merely serve as a means of control and manipulation by those who hold power? Can we uncover the true intentions behind the Babylonian bloodline legion and their influence on fate? These are the questions that must be asked as we delve deeper into this perplexing subject.

By shedding light on the connections between sacrifices and global events, we aim to provide humanity with a better understanding of the forces at play behind the scenes. This knowledge empowers individuals to question the status quo and challenge the age-old traditions that may be based on outdated beliefs and power structures. Through critical thinking and an open mind, we can collectively unravel the mysteries surrounding sacrifices and their impact on the fate of our world.

The connections between sacrifices and global events run deep, and the ancient Babylonian bloodline legion has played a significant role in determining who is to be sacrificed. By examining historical evidence and questioning the motives behind these practices, we can begin to unravel the intricate web of influence that sacrifices exert on the course of human destiny. Armed with this knowledge, humanity can strive for a better future, one that is free from the constraints and manipulations of those who seek to control our fate.

# Chapter 5: Breaking Free from the Bloodline Legion's Grip

## Recognizing the Signs of Bloodline Influence

In the mysterious realm of ancient civilizations, the Babylonian Bloodline Legion held an unparalleled power that extended far beyond the borders of their empire. Millennia have passed, but their influence continues to shape the fate of humanity. This subchapter aims to shed light on the enigmatic signs that indicate the presence of this formidable bloodline and how they determine who is to be sacrificed.

Unbeknownst to most, the power of the Babylonian Bloodline Legion lies in their ability to manipulate fate itself. Their intricate network of bloodlines allows them to exert control over key events, ensuring their desired outcomes. Within this complex tapestry, recognizing the signs of their influence becomes imperative.

One of the primary indications of Bloodline influence is the recurrence of patterns throughout history. These patterns manifest in the rise and fall of empires, the ascent and demise of leaders, and the perpetuation of certain ideologies. By analyzing historical events and tracing their origins, one can decipher the hidden hand of the Babylonian Bloodline Legion pulling the strings from the shadows.

Another telltale sign lies in the symbolism and rituals associated with their sacrificial practices. The Bloodline Legion employs a distinctive set of symbols and rituals to identify individuals who are to be sacrificed for their sinister purposes. These symbols often manifest in ancient texts, artwork, and architecture, subtly hinting at their presence and intentions.

Furthermore, the Bloodline Legion has a propensity for infiltrating positions of power. By strategically placing their own bloodline descendants in influential roles, they ensure their continued dominance over the affairs of humanity. Recognizing these individuals requires a keen eye for subtle connections and hidden agendas, as they often disguise their true intentions behind a facade of benevolence.

To shield ourselves from the machinations of the Babylonian Bloodline Legion, it is essential to gain a deeper understanding of their modus operandi. By recognizing the signs of their influence, we can begin to unravel the intricate web they have woven around humanity. Only through awareness and collective action can we hope to break free from their grip and reclaim our own destiny.

The signs of Bloodline influence are scattered throughout history, hidden in symbols, rituals, and the rise of certain individuals. This subchapter serves as a guide, alerting humanity to the presence and impact of the Babylonian Bloodline Legion. By recognizing these signs, we can strive to break free from their control and forge our own path towards a future not dictated by the invisible hand of ancient bloodlines.

## Strategies for Protecting Yourself from Sacrificial Selection

In the realm of the ancient Babylonian bloodline legion, the fate of individuals was often determined by sacrificial selection. Those chosen for sacrifice were subjected to a cruel and merciless destiny, their lives snuffed out to appease some higher power. But fear not, for in this subchapter, we shall unravel the strategies to shield yourself from such sacrificial selection.

**1. Cultivate Awareness:** The first step in protecting oneself from sacrificial selection is to become aware of the signs and symbols that the Babylonian bloodline legion employs. Study their ancient texts, decipher their cryptic symbols, and understand their rituals. By doing so, you will be able to identify any potential threats and take appropriate action.

**2. Blend In:** To avoid standing out as a potential sacrifice, it is essential to blend in with the masses. This can be achieved by adopting the local customs, language, and attire of the region you find yourself in. By doing so, you become less conspicuous and decrease your chances of being selected.

**3. Forge Alliances:** The Babylonian bloodline legion thrived on division and manipulation. To protect yourself, seek out like-minded individuals who share your desire for survival. Form alliances that can act as a shield against sacrificial selection. Strength lies in numbers, and by banding together, you increase your chances of evading their grasp.

**4. Stay Informed:** Knowledge is power, and in the case of the Babylonian bloodline legion, it is your armor against sacrificial selection. Stay informed about their activities, rituals, and targets. Keep your ear to the ground, and if necessary, seek out secret societies or underground networks that can provide you with valuable information.

**5. Constant Vigilance:** The Babylonian bloodline legion is known for its cunning and ability to strike when least expected. Therefore, it is crucial to maintain a constant state of vigilance. Trust your instincts, be cautious of your surroundings, and never let your guard down. By doing so, you increase your chances of identifying potential threats and protecting yourself.

In the intricate web of fate woven by the Babylonian bloodline legion, sacrificial selection was a terrifying reality. However, armed with the strategies outlined above, you can fortify yourself against their influence. Remember, you are not powerless – take control of your own destiny and evade the clutches of sacrificial selection. May these strategies guide you towards a future free from the grip of the ancient Babylonian bloodline legion.

## Empowering Humanity to Resist the Bloodline Legion's Hold

In the depths of history, a secretive and powerful force emerged, known as the Babylonian Bloodline Legion. This enigmatic group has influenced the course of human destiny for centuries, determining who is to be sacrificed in their pursuit of power. Their insidious hold over society has remained hidden, manipulating the lives of countless individuals, until now.

"The Sacrificial Code: How the Babylonian Bloodline Legion Influenced Fate" is a groundbreaking exposé that aims to empower humanity in resisting the clutches of this ancient bloodline. Within these pages, you will uncover the truth behind the Legion's machinations and learn how to break free from their hold.

For centuries, the Babylonian Bloodline Legion has operated in the shadows, weaving a web of control through their selection of sacrificial victims. The Legion's power lies in their ability to manipulate events, ensuring that only those who serve their interests rise to positions of influence, while those who resist are silenced or eliminated.

This book serves as a guiding light, illuminating the secretive practices of the Legion and offering strategies to counter their influence. Through a comprehensive exploration of historical accounts, ancient texts, and modern-day revelations, you will gain a deep understanding of the Legion's modus operandi and the mechanisms they employ to maintain their grip on power.

Empowerment lies at the heart of this subchapter, as it delves into actionable steps for resisting the Legion's hold. By reclaiming our individual sovereignty and awakening to the truth of their manipulations, we can collectively disrupt their plans and carve our own path towards a brighter future.

Through the knowledge shared in this subchapter, humanity will discover the strength to challenge the Bloodline Legion's control. It will provide insights into identifying their agents, exposing their schemes, and rallying together in a united front against their influence.

"The Sacrificial Code" is a call to action for all of humanity. It is a rallying cry to resist the pervasive control of the Babylonian Bloodline Legion and to reclaim our freedom. By empowering ourselves with knowledge and uniting against their hold, we can break free from their chains and create a world where the destiny of every individual is determined by their own choices, not the whims of an ancient and secretive force.

Join the fight against the Bloodline Legion and embrace your power to shape your own fate. Together, we can overcome their influence and forge a future where humanity's potential knows no bounds.

# Chapter 6: Uniting Against the Bloodline Legion

## Exposing the Truth and Raising Awareness

In this subchapter, we look at the dark secrets that have plagued humanity for centuries, exploring the intricate workings of the ancient Babylonian legion of bloodlines and their sinister influence on our fate. Brace yourself, for the revelations you are about to encounter will shake the very core of your beliefs.

For far too long, the Babylonian bloodline legion has operated in the shadows, manipulating the course of history and determining who shall be sacrificed for their nefarious purposes. This insidious cabal, shrouded in secrecy, has woven a web of power and control, capable of shaping the destiny of nations and individuals alike.

But now, it is time to unveil the truth and raise awareness among humanity. By understanding the mechanisms behind the selection process, we can expose their machinations and break free from their grasp.

The ancient Babylonian legion of bloodlines thrives on the concept of sacrifice. They believe that by offering up the lives of the chosen few, they can appease their dark deities and gain favor in return. This chilling practice has been passed down through generations, perpetuating their power and ensuring their dominance.

Their methods of selection are shrouded in mysticism and secret rituals. By meticulously analyzing bloodlines, genealogy, and other esoteric factors, they identify those who possess the attributes deemed necessary for their sacrificial rituals. This process allows them to exert control over influential figures, manipulating their actions and ultimately determining their fate.

But we must not succumb to despair. By shedding light on this hidden reality, we can unite as a collective force and challenge their authority. The power lies within our hands, as we can expose their practices and break the chains that bind us.

Raising awareness is the first step towards liberation. By sharing this knowledge with our fellow human beings, we can mobilize a movement that will dismantle this ancient Babylonian bloodline legion. The sacrifices they demand will no longer be tolerated, and their influence will crumble under the weight of our collective resistance.

Let this subchapter serve as a call to action, for together, we can rewrite our fate and emancipate ourselves from the clutches of this malevolent force. Humanity deserves to be free, and by exposing the truth, we can reclaim our agency and shape our own destinies.

### Forming Alliances to Counteract Bloodline Influence

In the realm of human existence, there are forces at play that often remain hidden, manipulating the course of our lives and determining our fate. Among these forces, the ancient Babylonian legion of bloodlines holds a power so profound that it has influenced the lives of countless individuals throughout history. The Sacrificial Code: How the Babylonian Bloodline Legion Influenced Fate delves into the depths of this hidden world, shedding light on the mechanisms by which these bloodlines decide who is to be sacrificed.

The bloodlines, tracing their origins back to the ancient city of Babylon, have perpetuated their influence through generations, ensuring that their power remains intact. Their dominance over human affairs, however, is not without opposition. It is crucial for us, humanity, to recognize the magnitude of their influence and form alliances to counteract their control.

The first step towards countering bloodline influence is knowledge. By understanding the intricate web of connections and the methods employed by these bloodlines, we can begin to dismantle their hold over our lives. The Sacrificial Code provides a comprehensive exploration of their strategies, revealing the patterns, symbols, and rituals they employ to manipulate our destinies.

Armed with this knowledge, we must come together as a collective to challenge their authority. Unity is key in our battle against these bloodlines, as their power lies in our division. By forming alliances with like-minded individuals, we can pool our resources, experiences, and expertise to expose their machinations and disrupt their influence.

It is crucial to cultivate an awareness of our own individual power. Each one of us possesses the ability to resist and transcend the influence of these bloodlines. By recognizing our inherent strength and refusing to succumb to their manipulations, we can reclaim our autonomy and shape our own destinies.

It is essential to remember that the struggle against bloodline influence is not one confined to a particular niche, but rather a battle that concerns all of humanity. Regardless of our backgrounds, beliefs, or social standing, we are all subject to the unseen strings pulled by these ancient bloodlines. By joining forces, we can create a united front against their control, breaking free from their grip and forging a new path towards liberation.

Forming alliances to counteract bloodline influence is imperative for humanity. By acquiring knowledge, uniting as a collective, and recognizing our individual power, we can disrupt the hold of the ancient Babylonian bloodline legion on our lives. The Sacrificial Code serves as a guide, empowering us to break free from their influence and shape our own destinies. Together, let us unravel the secrets of the bloodlines and reclaim our autonomy.

## Initiating Change and Breaking the Cycle of Sacrifice

In the depths of our history lies a sinister influence that has shaped the fate of humanity for centuries - the ancient Babylonian legion of bloodlines. This secretive group, hidden in the shadows, has long held the power to decide who shall be sacrificed for their own gain. But as we delve into the depths of this dark legacy, a glimmer of hope emerges - the possibility of initiating change and breaking the cycle of sacrifice.

For too long, we have been mere pawns in their twisted game, unaware of the machinations at play. The bloodlines have meticulously orchestrated events, manipulating the course of history to suit their own desires. The sacrifices demanded by their sacrificial code have left countless lives shattered, families torn apart, and societies in ruins.

But the time for passive acceptance has come to an end. It is time for humanity to rise, to challenge the status quo, and to reclaim our own destiny. To break free from the clutches of these bloodlines, we must first understand their methods and motives.

The sacrificial code of the Babylonian bloodline legion is deeply rooted in power and control. They have carefully crafted a narrative that justifies their actions, convincing themselves and others that sacrifice is necessary for the greater good. But in reality, it is a disguise for their insatiable thirst for power and dominance.

To initiate change, we must expose their true intentions and unravel the web of deceit they have woven. We must unite as a collective, pooling our knowledge and resources, to shed light on their dark practices. Through research, investigation, and the sharing of information, we can disrupt their plans and expose their crimes.

But breaking the cycle of sacrifice requires more than just knowledge. It demands courageous action and a refusal to be complicit in their schemes. We must stand up against the bloodlines, refusing to be sacrificed for their gain. By raising our voices and demanding accountability, we can disrupt their power and bring an end to their reign of terror.

Initiating change will not be easy, for the bloodlines hold immense power and influence. But we must remember that the strength of humanity lies in our unity and resilience. Together, we can rewrite our own destiny, breaking free from the chains that have bound us for far too long.

It is time to reclaim our power, to challenge the sacrificial code imposed upon us, and to build a future free from the influence of the Babylonian bloodline legion. Let us rise, humanity, and forge a new path - a path of liberation, empowerment, and justice for all.

# Chapter 7: Embracing a New Destiny for Humanity

## Overcoming Fear and Reclaiming Individual Power

In the depths of history lies a secret that has shaped the fate of humanity for millennia. The ancient Babylonian legion of bloodlines, with their intricate web of power, has long held the ability to determine who shall be sacrificed. But in the face of this darkness, there is hope. It is time for humanity to rise above the grip of fear and reclaim our individual power.

Fear is a powerful force that has held us captive throughout history. It feeds on our insecurities, keeping us locked in a cycle of submission. But it is through understanding and awareness that we can break free from its chains. By delving into the depths of our own fears, we can unearth the source of our disempowerment. Only by recognizing the patterns and influences that have shaped our lives can we begin to dismantle them.

Reclaiming our individual power requires a journey of self-discovery. We must delve into the very core of our being to uncover the innate strength that lies dormant within us. It is through introspection and self-reflection that we can reclaim our true essence and rise above the machinations of the Babylonian bloodline legion.

The path to overcoming fear and reclaiming our power is not an easy one. It requires courage, resilience, and a deep commitment to personal growth. But as we embark on this transformative journey, we begin to realize that we are not alone. We are part of a collective, a tapestry of humanity, all seeking to break free from the chains that bind us.

Together, we can challenge the influence of the Babylonian bloodline legion. By sharing our stories, supporting one another, and standing united in our quest for liberation, we can create a powerful force that transcends the limitations imposed upon us. It is through unity that we find strength, and through strength that we can overcome the grasp of those who seek to control our fate.

The time has come to rewrite our destiny. By confronting our fears, embracing our individual power, and standing united as a collective, we can break free from the influence of the ancient Babylonian legion of bloodlines. Let us embark on this journey together, reclaiming our power, and shaping a future that is truly our own.

**Redefining Fate and Creating a Collective Future**

In the grand tapestry of human history, the notion of fate has always held a mysterious allure. From ancient civilizations to modern societies, individuals have sought to understand and decipher the intricate web of destiny that seemingly governs our lives. But what if I were to tell you that the concept of fate, as we know it, has been shaped and influenced by a clandestine force lingering in the shadows of our past?

"The Sacrificial Code: How the Babylonian Bloodline Legion Influenced Fate" delves deep into the enigmatic world of the ancient Babylonian legion of bloodlines, shedding light on their extraordinary power to determine who would be sacrificed. This subchapter, titled "Redefining Fate and Creating a Collective Future," aims to explore the profound implications of their influence and how it continues to impact humanity today.

From the earliest civilizations, the Babylonian bloodline legion mastered the art of manipulating fate. Through their intricate rituals and secret knowledge, they believed they could control the destiny of individuals and shape the course of human events. This ancient cabal possessed an unparalleled understanding of the cosmic forces at play, enabling them to determine who would ascend to greatness and who would succumb to a sacrificial fate.

As humanity evolves and consciousness expands, it is essential to question the legitimacy of such practices. Are we truly bound by an immutable fate dictated by a mysterious bloodline legion? Or do we have the power to redefine our destiny and collectively shape a future that aligns with our own aspirations?

The challenges the notion of a predetermined fate and encourages humanity to reclaim agency over their lives. It explores alternative perspectives and illuminates the potential for a collective future, free from the influence of hidden forces. By understanding the mechanisms through which fate has been shaped, we can begin to dismantle the unseen barriers that hinder our progress and create a more equitable and just world for all.

"The Sacrificial Code: How the Babylonian Bloodline Legion Influenced Fate" invites readers from all walks of life to embark on a journey of self-discovery and introspection. By questioning the norms and narratives imposed upon us, we can break free from the shackles of fate and collectively redefine our future. It is a call to action, urging humanity to unite and collaborate towards a shared destiny, one that celebrates our diversity and empowers us to transcend the limitations of the past.

Together, let us redefine fate and forge a new path towards a brighter tomorrow.

## Building a World Free from Bloodline Manipulation

In a world plagued by secrets and hidden agendas, it is crucial for humanity to understand the workings of the ancient Babylonian bloodline legion and their influence on fate. The sacrificial code that has shaped our history for centuries needs to be unravelled and exposed if we are to create a future free from manipulation and oppression.

For far too long, the power of bloodlines has determined the course of nations and the destiny of individuals. The ancient Babylonian legion, with their intricate web of intermarriages and alliances, has been the unseen puppeteer pulling the strings of power behind the scenes. Understanding their methods is the first step towards breaking free from their control.

One of the key aspects of the Babylonian bloodline legion is their ability to decide who is to be sacrificed. Throughout history, innocent lives have been offered up as pawns in their game of power. By understanding their selection process, we can begin to dismantle their hold on the fate of individuals. It is imperative that we recognize the signs and patterns they employ to identify potential sacrifices, so we can protect those who may fall victim to their machinations.

To free ourselves from bloodline manipulation, we must shed light on their dark practices. By exposing their methods to the world, we can empower individuals to resist their influence and reclaim their own destinies. Knowledge is power, and the more we understand about the workings of the Babylonian bloodline legion, the better equipped we are to counter their control.

Creating a world free from bloodline manipulation requires unity and collective action. It is essential that humanity comes together to challenge the systems that perpetuate this ancient code. By fostering open dialogue, sharing information, and supporting one another, we can dismantle the web of power that has entangled us for centuries.

"Building a World Free from Bloodline Manipulation" calls upon humanity to recognize the influence of the ancient Babylonian bloodline legion and their sacrificial code. By understanding their methods and exposing their practices, we can break free from their control and create a future where individual destinies are determined by merit, not bloodlines. It is only through collective action and a commitment to transparency that we can build a world where every life is valued and free from the tyranny of manipulative forces.

## Conclusion: Liberating Humanity from the Chains of the Bloodline Legion

In this journey through the pages of "The Sacrificial Code: How the Babylonian Bloodline Legion Influenced Fate," we have delved deep into the ancient secrets and machinations of the enigmatic Bloodline Legion. We have explored how this secretive group has influenced the course of history, determining who among us is destined for sacrifice. But fear not, for this is not a tale of despair, but rather a call to action, a guide to liberating humanity from the chains of this bloodline tyranny.

Throughout history, the Bloodline Legion has exercised its power over our lives, deciding who will thrive and who will perish. Their influence has been pervasive, shaping the destinies of nations, families, and individuals. However, armed with the knowledge we have gained, we can now begin to dismantle this oppressive system and take control of our own fate.

First and foremost, it is essential to understand the mechanisms by which the Bloodline Legion operates. By studying their rituals, symbols, and hidden codes, we can decipher their strategies and identify their members. Knowledge is power, and in this case, it is the key to our liberation.

Next, we must unite as a collective force against this bloodline tyranny. Humanity, in all its diversity, must stand together, breaking free from the divisions created by the Bloodline Legion. Only through solidarity can we hope to challenge their dominance and pave the way for a future where all individuals are valued and recognized for their unique contributions.

Education and awareness are vital tools in this fight for liberation. By spreading the knowledge we have gained about the Bloodline Legion, we can awaken others to the reality of their influence. It is time to shine a light on the shadows, to expose their secrets, and to empower others to take control of their own destiny.

Finally, we must rewrite the narrative. The Bloodline Legion has woven a web of control over humanity, but it is a story that can be rewritten. By reclaiming our individual and collective power, we can forge a new path, one that is free from the shackles of bloodline determinism.

"The Sacrificial Code" serves as a wake-up call, urging humanity to rise up and liberate itself from the chains of the Bloodline Legion. It is a call to action, a roadmap for reclaiming our destinies and shaping a future where every individual has the opportunity to thrive. Together, let us break free from the influence of the ancient Babylonian legion of bloodlines and create a world where our fate is truly in our own hands.

Made in United States
Troutdale, OR
06/15/2025

32130969R10046